Jakob & Wilhelm
Grimm

Editors: Ann Redpath, Etienne Delessert
Art Director: Rita Marshall
Publisher: George R. Peterson, Jr.

Copyright © 1984 Creative Education, Inc., 123 S. Broad Street,
Mankato, Minnesota 56001, USA. American Edition.
Copyright © 1984 Grasset & Fasquelle, Paris – Editions 24 Heures, Lausanne. French Edition.
International copyrights reserved in all countries.

Library of Congress Catalog Card No.: 83-71186
Grimm, Jakob and Wilhelm; The Queen Bee
Mankato, MN: Creative Education, Inc.; 32 pages. ISBN: 0-87191-939-7

Color separations by Photolitho A.G., Gossau/Zurich
Printed in Switzerland by Imprimeries Réunies S.A. Lausanne.

# THE QUEENBEE

JAKOB & WILHELM GRIMM
illustrated by
PHILIPPE DUMAS

CREATIVE EDUCATION INC.

# ONCE UPON A TIME

TWO Princes started off in search of adventure, and, falling into a wild, free way of life, did not come home again.

The third Brother, the youngest, set out to look for the other two. But when at last he found them, they mocked him for thinking he could make his way in the world with his simplicity, while they, who were so much more clever, could not get on.

All three went on together till they came to an anthill. The two elder Princes wanted to disturb it, to see how the little ants crept away, carrying their eggs.

But the third Prince said: "Leave the little creature alone. I will not allow you to disturb them."

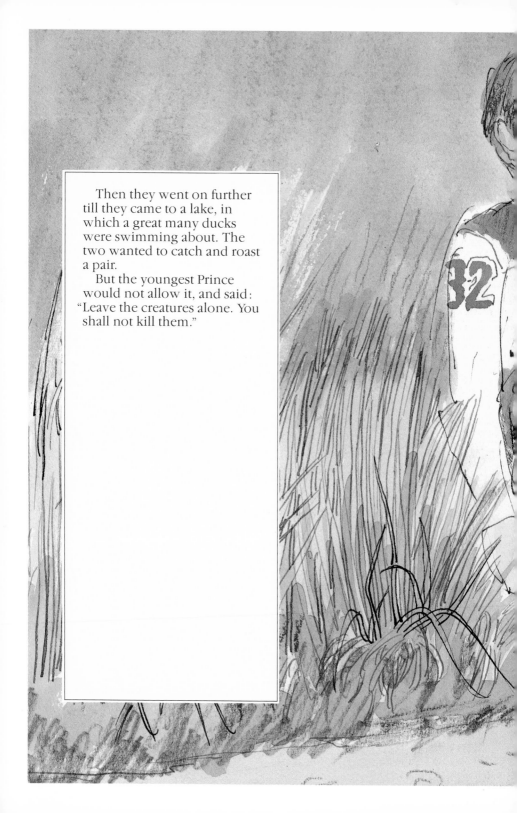

Then they went on further
till they came to a lake, in
which a great many ducks
were swimming about. The
two wanted to catch and roast
a pair.

But the youngest Prince
would not allow it, and said:
"Leave the creatures alone. You
shall not kill them."

At last they came to a bees' nest, containing such a quantity of honey that it flowed round the trunk of the tree.

The two Princes wanted to set fire to the tree, and suffocate the bees, so as to remove the honey.

But the youngest Prince stopped them again, and said: "Leave the creatures alone. I will not let you burn them."

At last the three Brothers came to a castle, where the stables were full of stone horses, but not a soul was to be seen. They went through all the rooms till they came to a door quite at the end, fastened with three bolts. In the middle of the door was a lattice, through which one could see into the room.

There they saw a little grey
man sitting at a table. They
called to him once—twice—
but he did not hear them.
Finally, when they had called
him the third time, he stood
up and opened the door, and
came out. He said not a word,
but led them to a richly spread
table, and when they had eaten
and drunk, he took them each
to a bedroom.

The next morning the little
grey man came to the eldest
Prince, beckoned, and led him
to a stone tablet whereon were
inscribed three tasks by means
of which the castle should be
freed from enchantment.

This was the first task: In the wood, under the moss, lay the Princesses' pearls, a thousand in number. These had to all be found, and if at sunset a single one were missing, the seeker would be turned to stone.

The eldest went away, and searched all day, but when evening came, he had only found the first hundred, and it happened as the inscription foretold. He was turned to stone.

The next day the second Brother undertook the quest. But he fared no better than the first, for he only found two hundred pearls, and he too was turned to stone.

At last the third Brother's turn came. He searched in the moss, but the pearls were hard to find, and he worked slowly.

Then he sat down on a rock and cried. But as he was sitting there, the Ant King, whose life he had saved, came up with five thousand ants, and it was not long before the little creatures had found all the pearls and laid them in a heap.

Now the second task was to get the key of the Princesses' room out of the lake.

When the youngest Prince came to the lake, the ducks he had once saved swam up, dived, and brought up the key from the depths.

But the third task was the hardest. The Prince had to find out which was the youngest and most charming of the Princesses while they were asleep.

They were exactly alike, and could not be distinguished in any way, except that before going to sleep, each had eaten a different kind of sweet. The eldest had a piece of sugar, the second a little syrup, and the youngest a spoonful of honey.

Then the Queen of the Bees, whom the youngest Prince had saved from burning, came and tasted the lips of all three. She settled on the mouth of the one who had eaten the honey, and so the Prince recognized the right one.

Then the charm was broken
and everything in the castle
was set free, and those who
had been turned to stone took
human form again.

And the youngest Prince
married the youngest and
sweetest Princess, and became
King after her father's death,
while his two Brothers married
the other sisters.